the
Lollipop Fairy
A SWEET BIRTHDAY TRADITION

Hardcover: 978-0-578-31705-2
Paperback: 978-0-578-33061-7
E-Book: 978-0-578-37391-1

Library of Congress Control Number: 2021923115

First edition January, 2022.

Cover art & Illustrations: Riley Helal
Editor: John Briggs
Layout by: Jana M. Anderson & Riley Helal

Printed in China.

The Birthday Tradition

1. Lollipop Seeds arrive
2. Read story together
3. Plant seeds by midnight
4. Wake up to a lollipop garden on your birthday

In all the world
there is no one like you.
You are dearly **loved**
all year through.

But tomorrow is your **special** day.

That one moment in the year
we call your **birthday.**

A day that is all about you.
A day that tells us how much you grew.
So, with **excitement** we say . . .

The Lollipop Fairy is on her way
to help you celebrate her **favorite** day:

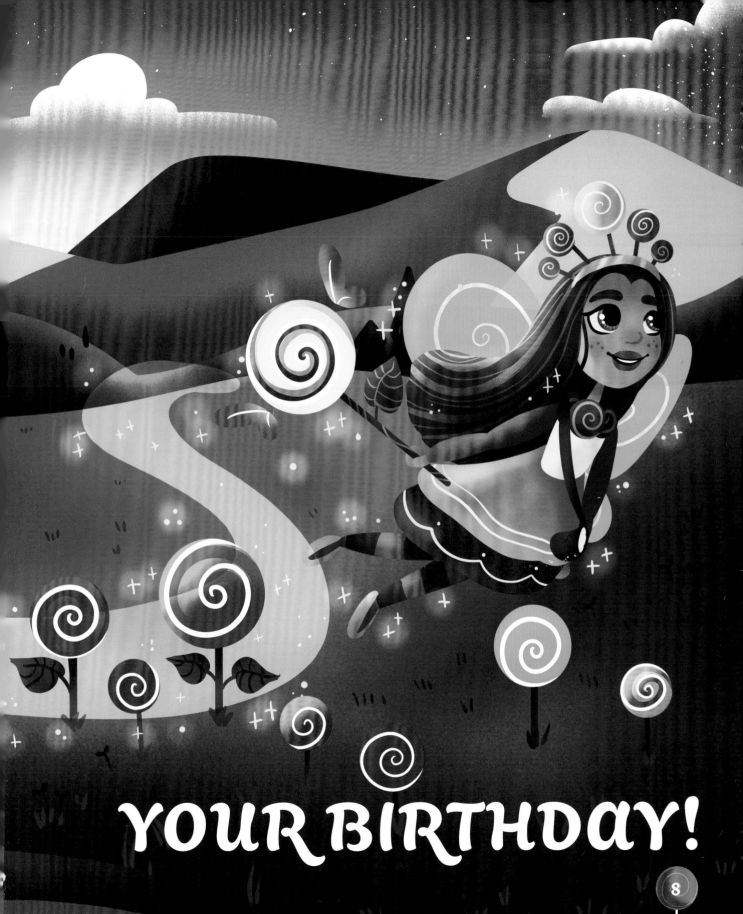

YOUR BIRTHDAY!

The **lollipop** seeds have arrived
for you to plant far and wide.

One seed per year
makes each lollipop appear.

Sow your seeds.
Get ready for bed,

and **dream** about your day ahead.

Sleep well.
Sleep tight.
Tomorrow you will awake
to a lollipop **delight.**

14

Are you turning **1, 2, 3** or **4?**

There is **always** one more lollipop
than the year before.

5, 6, 7 or 8?

So many sweet, delicious lollipops
I can hardly wait!

Whether they are red, yellow, orange or blue,
or a **colorful** swirl of more than two,

each one means
another **year** here

18

and one more reason

for all of us to

CHEER!

Enjoy your **sugar** swirls.
Enjoy your special day.

Goodbye, Lollipop Fairy.

One more year
until you are
back this way!

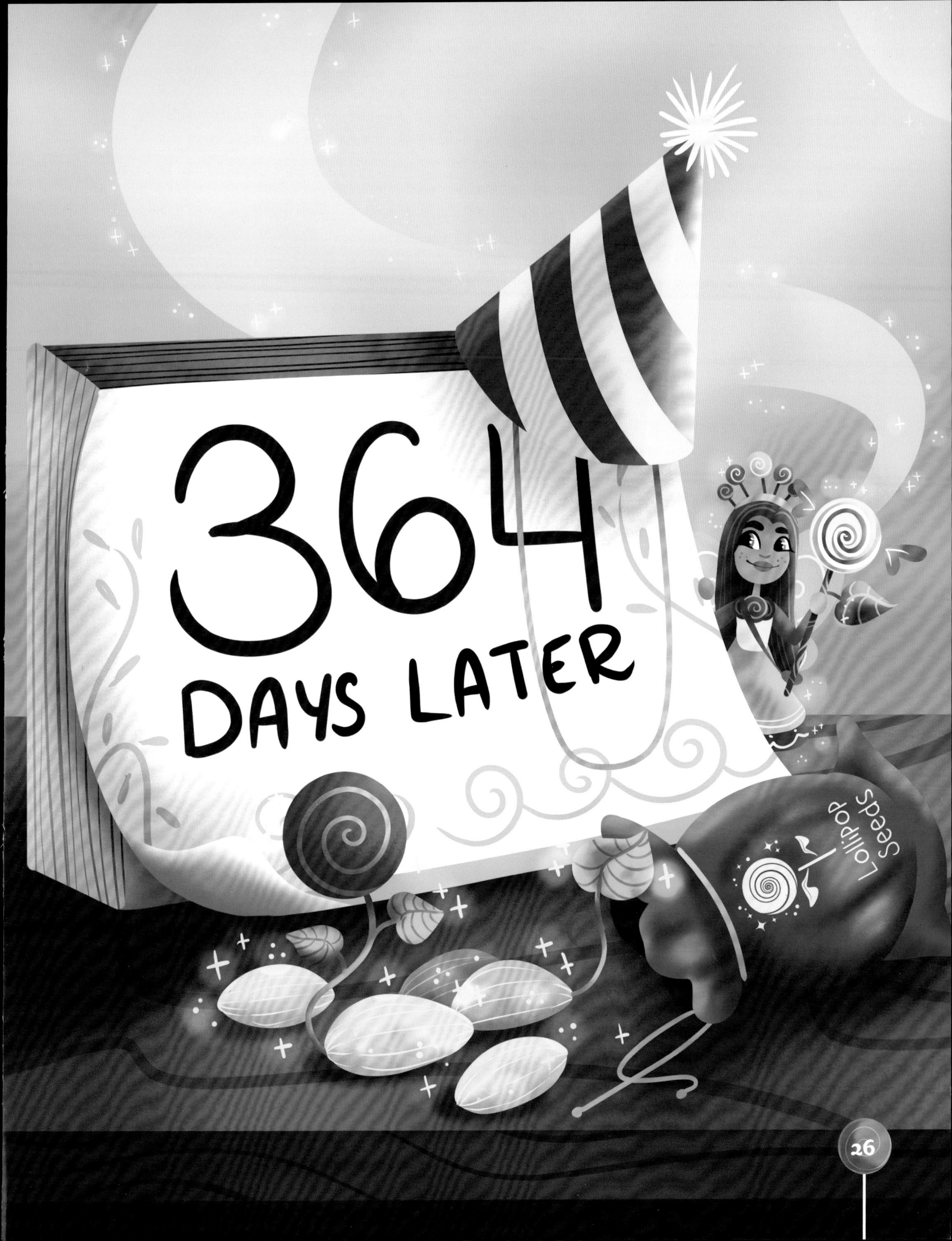
364
DAYS LATER
Lollipop Seeds

The Lollipop Fairy Tradition in Our Home Over the Years

To my sons, Alex and Collin,
You will always be the greatest joy
and sweetness in my life.
Love,
Mom

27

Jana M. Anderson is a literacy specialist, Special-Education teacher, and mother of two sons and two lazy labradors. She has been a lifelong advocate for children with different needs.

Jana attended the University of North Texas where she earned a bachelor's degree in Elementary and Special Education and a master's degree in Special Education.

She and her family reside in San Diego, California, and 17 years later, they still enjoy this sweet family tradition. For more information about the author, please visit www.lollipopfairy.com

Riley Helal is an illustrator and graphic designer who resides in Coeur d'Alene, Idaho. She loves drawing magic, monsters and all things fun. For more information about the illustrator, please visit www.rileyhelal.myportfolio.com